Libraries and Information

1 8 AUG 2021

ᴡꜰ 1/24

This book should be returned by the last date stamped above.
You may renew the loan personally, by post or telephone for a
further period if the book is not required by another reader.

www.wakefield.gov.uk

wakefieldcouncil
working for you

To Sasha and Liza x

First published in 2020 by Child's Play (International) Ltd
Ashworth Road, Bridgemead, Swindon SN5 7YD, UK

First published in USA in 2020 by Child's Play Inc
250 Minot Avenue, Auburn, Maine 04210

Distributed in Australia by Child's Play Australia Pty Ltd
Unit 10/20 Narabang Way, Belrose, Sydney, NSW 2085

Text copyright © 2020 Susan Rollings
Illustrations copyright © 2020 Child's Play (International)
The moral rights of the author and illustrator have been asserted

ISBN 978-1-78628-465-5
SJ200320CPL04204655

Printed in Shenzhen, China

1 3 5 7 9 10 8 6 4 2

A catalogue record of this book
is available from the British Library

www.childs-play.com

Best Friends, Busy Friends

Susan Rollings   illustrated by Nichola Cowdery

Our friends, best friends,

those who wake us up friends!

Busy friends, helpful friends,

time to go to school friends.

Slow friends,

fast friends,

running around the playground friends.

Tall friends,

small friends,

learning how to read friends.

Tidy friends,

messy friends,

kind and very caring friends.

Singing friends, dancing friends,

hopping, skipping, jumping friends!

Funny friends, silly friends,

sometimes not so kind friends!

Wet friends,

swimming friends,

splashing in the water friends.

Still friends,

quiet friends,

reading us a story friends.

Sad friends,

happy friends,

skipping home from school friends.

Furry friends,

feathered friends,

lots of very hungry friends!

Our friends, happy friends,

home and after school friends.

Fluffy friends, nosy friends,

off to meet important friends.

Best friends, special friends,

surprise, surprise! It's all our friends!

book belongs to:

. . . .

igloobooks

Published in 2017
by Igloo Books Ltd
Cottage Farm
Sywell
NN6 0BJ
www.igloobooks.com

Written by Melanie Joyce
Illustrated by César Samaniego

Designed by Amy Bradford
Edited by Kathryn Beer

STA002 1117
2 4 6 8 10 9 7 5 3 1
ISBN 978-1-78810-153-0

Printed and manufactured in China

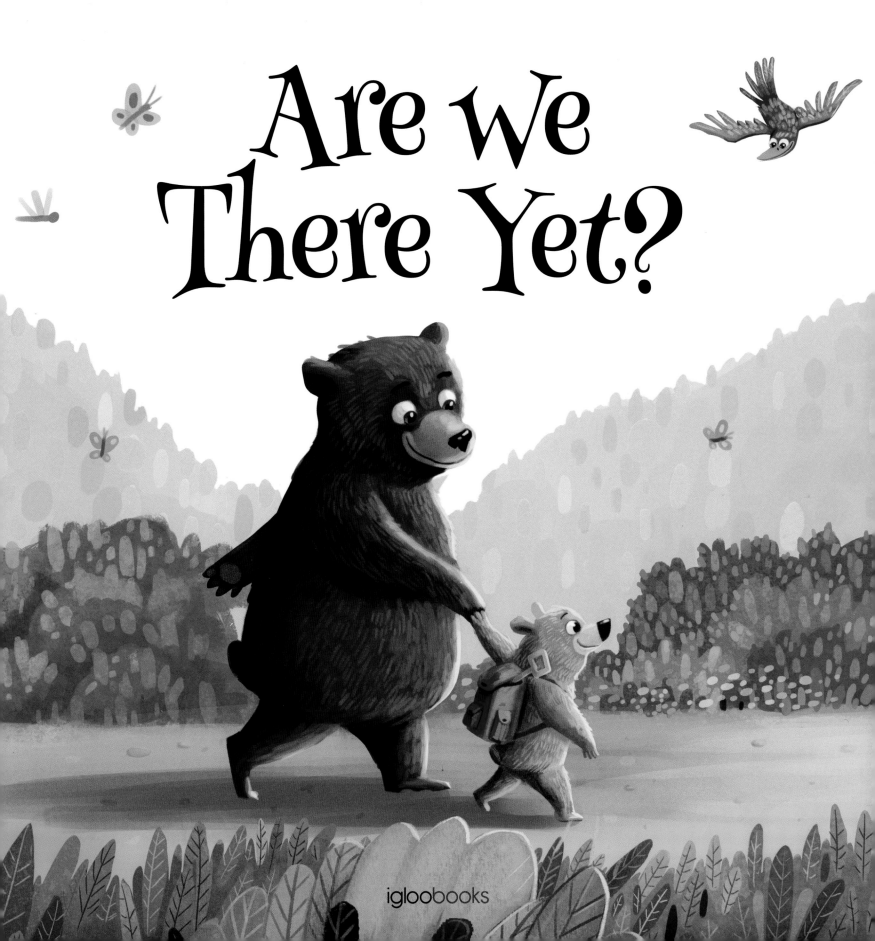

Are We There Yet?

igloobooks

Once there was a little bear who longed to go to the sea.
One sunny morning he said,

Please, Daddy will you take me?

"Alright," said Daddy. "Go and get ready, the sea is quite a long way."

Little Bear jumped up and down.

I'm off to the sea. Hooray!

Mummy rolled up Little Bear's dolphin towel and put it in his pack.

He stuffed in his bucket and spade, then followed Daddy down the track.

Little Bear raced ahead, as fast as his paws could go.

Daddy laughed and said, "There's a long way to go yet, Little Bear."
But suddenly Little Bear shouted,

I can see the sea over there!

"That's only a stream," said Daddy. "The sea is big and blue. There are noisy birds and sand, and little seashells, too."

Little Bear and Daddy went through the forest and over the hill.

On and on they plodded past squirrels and rabbits until...

Then suddenly they arrived at a big, blue shiny lake.

"It's the sea!" shouted Little Bear,
with an excited cry.

No it isn't,

quacked the ducks as they went swimming by.

"Be patient a little bit longer," said Daddy to the disappointed bear. But Little Bear was wondering...

Will we ever really get there?

Friendly foxes with surf boards, waved and said, "Hello."

Have fun at the sea! they cried.

It's not too far to go.

Little Bear was terribly excited to think he was getting so near.
But the sandy path went on and on, and the sea did not appear.

NOTHING TO SEE HERE

Are we there yet?

asked Little Bear.

Daddy, when will it be?

But Daddy just smiled and pointed, because at last they had reached the...

Little Bear had never seen anything so wonderful before.
He let out a squeal of excitement and ran towards the shore.